MR. MISCHIEF
a spot of trouble

Original concept by Roger Hargreaves
Illustrated and written by Adam Hargreaves

MR. MEN   LITTLE MISS

Mr Mischief woke up and groaned.

He did not feel well.

In fact, he felt decidedly unwell.

He got up and went to the bathroom to look at himself in the mirror.

He was covered in spots!

So he made an appointment with
Dr Makeyouwell.

"You've got measles," said the Doctor, "and the best thing you can do is go home to bed and stay there for a week."

Mr Mischief's face fell.

A whole week in bed.

No mischief for a whole week!

Mr Mischief groaned for the second time that day.

"And don't forget," said Dr Makeyouwell as Mr Mischief was leaving, "measles are very catching."

Mr Mischief closed the door and then he grinned.

A very mischievous grin.

The sort of grin that meant that he was about to get up to no good.

Before he went home, Mr Mischief popped into the hardware shop and bought a pot of yellow paint.

Then he painted over all his spots, before paying Mr Happy a visit.

He didn't stay long, just long enough.

Long enough, thought Mr Mischief as he walked home, to give Mr Happy the measles!

When he got home he went to bed and lay there chuckling to himself. What a nasty person he is!

All the next day he lay in bed and thought about the trick he had played on Mr Happy.

And he thought, if Mr Happy had the measles, then Mr Tickle might catch them from Mr Happy.

Mr Mischief chuckled at the thought of
Mr Tickle with spots all over his long arms.

And Mr Nosey might catch the measles from Mr Tickle.

And he chuckled at the thought of Mr Nosey with a spotty nose.

And he chuckled at the thought of Mr Tall with spotty legs.

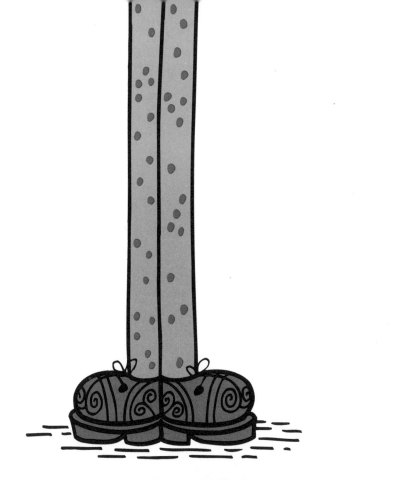

And Mr Wrong, who would probably have blue spots, because he gets everything wrong.

And Little Miss Tiny would only have room for one spot on her body.

"This will keep me happy all week long," chuckled Mr Mischief to himself.

Just then there was a knock at the door.

Mr Mischief struggled out of bed and answered it.

"Hello," said Mr Happy. "I heard you had the measles so I thought I'd come round and cheer you up. Here, I bought you these."

Mr Happy gave Mr Mischief a bunch of grapes.

Mr Mischief looked at Mr Happy, but as hard as he looked, he couldn't see any spots.

Not one!

"Aren't you afraid of catching the measles from me?" stammered Mr Mischief.

"Of course not," said Mr Happy, "I've already had them. And as you know, you can only get measles once!"

Mr Mischief's face fell and he groaned.

Again.

"What's wrong?" asked Mr Happy. "Don't you like grapes?"

3 Great Offers for MR.MEN Fans!

MR.MEN TOKEN

1 New Mr. Men or Little Miss Library Bus Presentation Cases

A brand new stronger, roomier school bus library box, with sturdy carrying handle and stay-closed fasteners.
The full colour, wipe-clean boxes make a great home for your full collection.
They're just £5.99 inc P&P and free bookmark!

☐ MR. MEN   ☐ LITTLE MISS (please tick and order overleaf)

2 Door Hangers and Posters

In every Mr. Men and Little Miss book like this one, you will find a special token. Collect 6 tokens and we will send you a brilliant Mr. Men or Little Miss poster and a Mr. Men or Little Miss double sided full colour bedroom door hanger of your choice. Simply tick your choice in the list and tape a 50p coin for your two items to this page.

PLEASE STICK YOUR 50P COIN HERE

Door Hangers (please tick)
☐ Mr. Nosey & Mr. Muddle
☐ Mr. Slow & Mr. Busy
☐ Mr. Messy & Mr. Quiet
☐ Mr. Perfect & Mr. Forgetful
☐ Little Miss Fun & Little Miss Late
☐ Little Miss Helpful & Little Miss Tidy
☐ Little Miss Busy & Little Miss Brainy
☐ Little Miss Star & Little Miss Fun

Posters (please tick)
☐ MR.MEN
☐ LITTLE MISS

3 Sixteen Beautiful Fridge Magnets – any 2 for £2.00!
inc.P&P

They're very special collector's items!
Simply tick your first and second* choices from the list below
of any 2 characters!

1st Choice

- [ ] Mr. Happy
- [ ] Mr. Lazy
- [ ] Mr. Topsy-Turvy
- [ ] Mr. Bounce
- [ ] Mr. Bump
- [ ] Mr. Small
- [ ] Mr. Snow
- [ ] Mr. Wrong
- [ ] Mr. Daydream
- [ ] Mr. Tickle
- [ ] Mr. Greedy
- [ ] Mr. Funny
- [ ] Little Miss Giggles
- [ ] Little Miss Splendid
- [ ] Little Miss Naughty
- [ ] Little Miss Sunshine

2nd Choice

- [ ] Mr. Happy
- [ ] Mr. Lazy
- [ ] Mr. Topsy-Turvy
- [ ] Mr. Bounce
- [ ] Mr. Bump
- [ ] Mr. Small
- [ ] Mr. Snow
- [ ] Mr. Wrong
- [ ] Mr. Daydream
- [ ] Mr. Tickle
- [ ] Mr. Greedy
- [ ] Mr. Funny
- [ ] Little Miss Giggles
- [ ] Little Miss Splendid
- [ ] Little Miss Naughty
- [ ] Little Miss Sunshine

*Only in case your first choice is out of stock.

TO BE COMPLETED BY AN ADULT

To apply for any of these great offers, ask an adult to complete the coupon below and send it with the appropriate payment and tokens, if needed, to MR. MEN OFFERS, PO BOX 7, MANCHESTER M19 2HD

- [ ] Please send _____ Mr. Men Library case(s) and/or_____ Little Miss Library case(s) at £5.99 each inc P&P
- [ ] Please send a poster and door hanger as selected overleaf. I enclose six tokens plus a 50p coin for P&P
- [ ] Please send me _____ pair(s) of Mr. Men/Little Miss fridge magnets, as selected above at £2.00 inc P&P

Fan's Name _____

Address _____

_____ **Postcode** _____

Date of Birth _____

Name of Parent/Guardian _____

Total amount enclosed £_____

- [ ] **I enclose a cheque/postal order payable to Egmont Books Limited**
- [ ] **Please charge my MasterCard/Visa/Amex/Switch or Delta account** (delete as appropriate)

Card Number

Expiry date ___/___ **Signature** _____

Please allow 28 days for delivery. We reserve the right to change the terms of this offer at any time but we offer a 14 day money back guarantee. This does not affect your statutory rights.

MR.MEN   LITTLE MISS
Mr. Men and Little Miss™ & ©Mrs. Roger Hargreaves

CUT ALONG DOTTED LINE AND RETURN THIS WHOLE PAGE